T0365912

THE
AUTHOR

CAROLANN PLANK

authorHOUSE®

AuthorHouse™
1663 Liberty Drive
Bloomington, IN 47403
www.authorhouse.com
Phone: 1 (800) 839-8640

Published by AuthorHouse 02/02/2017

ISBN: 978-1-5246-7042-9 (sc)
ISBN: 978-1-5246-7041-2 (e)

Print information available on the last page.

Any people depicted in stock imagery provided by Thinkstock are models,
and such images are being used for illustrative purposes only.
Certain stock imagery © Thinkstock.

This book is printed on acid-free paper.

Because of the dynamic nature of the Internet, any web addresses or
links contained in this book may have changed since publication and
may no longer be valid. The views expressed in this work are solely those
of the author and do not necessarily reflect the views of the publisher,
and the publisher hereby disclaims any responsibility for them.

Before you read The Author I would like to say a couple of things. First, I had this idea stirring in my mind for about two and a half years. From inception it has changed dramatically because The Author was originally going to be a play instead of a short story. Secondly, I would like to inform you that all characters are fictional and any resemblance in any way is entirely coincidental. Thank you for your support and enjoy the story.

Carolann Plank

I would like to thank my parents for giving

me the courage to bring this story to life

and everyone who has believed in me.

*I*t was a quiet October night, 1880, New York City during a time of great progress and changing mindsets. Much like the established people who populated the busy streets, the city itself was proud and thriving. The hustle and bustle of fortune seekers and bright-eyed dreamers settled this great American city. The rest of the nation had its eyes fixed on New York and the exceptional author that it had created in Yorkville.

William Warren had spent his childhood in a spacious mansion to accompany his lavish lifestyle in Long Island. His family was surprised when he downgraded to a three bedroom colonial house when he left home to pursue his writing career. Despite his wealthy roots, William preferred the cozy feeling of a two story home nestled on the outskirts of the busy city.

He lied on his back, the covers loosely draped over his slim body. The only sound that could be heard was his gentle, steady breathing. Though he did not stir, his mind and heart were racing. His dreams were haunted with sinister demons and monsters and things most would find disturbing and frightening. Not William. For him, the creatures that crawled and slithered around his brain sparked his twisted imagination, and when he was awake, he would scribble down these horrors in what would become a new bestseller.

From a young age William and everyone around him could plainly see his talent and encouraged him to pursue a career in writing. Being from a family with a sterling reputation and powerful connections, the Warrens were able to introduce their talented son to a publishing company in Philadelphia. William shared his short stories with the publishing company and after reading them, they immediately signed a contract to represent William.

The much lesser known apprentice, Eleanor Price,

who was deep in an obscure dream two rooms down from William, dreamt of escaping the shadow of her mentor and write her way to fame as he had. She was a girl of only twenty one. Her dark brown eyes and simple beauty allowed for an approachable and likeable presence. Her long honey blonde hair was always kept in a loose plait braid that ran down her back. Revered for her compliancy and continuous respect for him, William employed Eleanor as his assistant. He was not married nor did he have many friends, but still craved companionship. Romantic feelings for Eleanor never crossed his mind and it was obvious to William she was not seeking anything more than employment and his friendship.

As the months passed he began to see more and more of himself in the young girl. During her free time, he would see her writing and noticed the indent on her middle finger of her right hand caused by hours of relentlessly gripping a quill. Eleanor's only dream was to be a famous writer. She was graced with determination and intelligence. Eleanor did not have any friends. Her acquaintances were William's very limited number of friends and family. For most of their visits she would excuse herself, preferring her own company over tea and small talk. It was disconcerting for her to listen to William's family insist that he take a wife to share his success. That sort of talk exasperated Eleanor. She had never seen William take a particular liking to any woman he came across. Eleanor noticed the tireless lectures from his family to marry made him uncomfortable.

The sun moved boldly into the sky spreading golds and pinks to wake the city that never sleeps. Days are long when William sits wearily at the old but well-polished oak desk elegantly placed in the middle of his study.

Eleanor had sifted, sorted, and labeled the documents William had given her the day before and placed them neatly on the desk. As William was fully concentrated on his next bestseller, he hadn't noticed Eleanor's workload was not enough to consume the days beyond late afternoon. Eleanor did not mind, she would simply satisfy the remaining hours of the day with her own writings in hopes of turning it over to her mentor for praise. That day had finally arrived.

"May I come in?" Eleanor asked softly peaking inside the half-open door of his study. She noticed William was in a rather unusual position. Instead of sitting straight and leaning into his desk with his fingers frantically gliding over the keys of his treasured Remington Standard N0. 2 typewriter, his striking face rests buried in his slender arms. Without raising his head from the desk, William waves her in. Eleanor tried to hold back a satisfied smile of her most recent achievement. Rejection never crossed her mind as she looked down at the completed draft of her first novel. She knew it was good, quite good actually; perhaps even good enough to be pushed into publishing with a little help from William.

"There is something I would like you to read." Eleanor pushes the neatly tied papers closer to William. "If time permits of course."

He lifted his head with great struggle, his face pale and sunken. The wanderlust in his eyes was replaced by vibrant blood vessels and his sandy blonde hair had been matted over the course of the day by tiredly running his hands through it.

Taking a step back Eleanor softly stammered, "Sir, are you alright? You look ill." She set the papers on his desk, pulled an armless wooden chair next to him and touched his forehead to feel for signs of fever.

"I have lost my ability to write" he quietly states

gently pushing her hand aside. His hand pulls at the tangles in his tousled hair as he rakes his hands through them. "The bank of ideas I have drawn inspiration from for so many years has vanished; the dreams have ceased!"

The two sat in silence for several minutes before William's eyes fall on the pile of papers Eleanor had placed on his desk. With a sincere promise to read them, he sends her off without another word.

To understand the downfall of William Warren you must first understand the desperation of this man. There was nowhere to go but down in his career, he was at the peak, he had fame, loyal followers, and a salary sprouting from what he loved to do most. Constant visits from the publisher to track progress on his latest project put endless pressure on William to remain on top. Always looking for more and wanting William to produce another bestseller was starting to take its toll on him. When the thought of falling from the top started to creep into his mind, he began to collapse into a nightmare of nothingness.

William spent days in the comfort of his bed trying to conjure an idea that would trigger inspiration for his half written manuscript. William's behavior had shifted to hopelessness. He seemed lost and could not concentrate on simple tasks, including bathing and grooming. Eleanor began to worry; she was not accustomed to mothering the person she looked up to for guidance for the past 18 months. She tried to pick apart his mind to find the root of his torment that loomed over him like a storm cloud. As hard as she tried to understand, she couldn't figure out why the nightmares had ceased. Eleanor knew if William continued on this path he would soon become nothing more than a distant memory in the eye of his loyal readers. Eleanor was not ready to let that happen, at least not before she was made famous. She needed William to be more than a short-lived success story. Eleanor was counting on William to help her become a well renowned author. She craved recognition and fame and longed for the spotlight to show the world she was just as gifted as her mentor. Eleanor was feeling as desperate as William.

Early morning before the birds had begun to sing, Eleanor left a note for William, so not to wake him, saying she would be back within the week. She believed she had finally come up with a solution.

A heavily occupied train took Eleanor from New York City to northern New Hampshire. Nestled in a Victorian architecture home with three wide-eyed children and a devoted husband lived Margaret Price, older sister to Eleanor. It has been two years since Eleanor saw her sister. It was their mother's funeral that brought them together. A few months before Eleanor started to work for William she received a telegram announcing her mother had peacefully died in her sleep after succumbing to a long term illness. At the funeral, feelings of resentment towards her sister continued as Eleanor remained invisible while family and friends comforted Margaret.

For Eleanor, the reunion was less than glorious. The two were never close growing up. Margaret was favored by her parents. She was beautiful and refined in social settings and never failed to capture the center of attention. Eleanor was thin and timid. She felt uneasy at social events often sitting alone and watching her sister charming those that flocked around her. As expected by their parents, Margaret married a successful gentleman who was attentive to her needs and provided an extravagant life style. Eleanor never wanted to be a wife that was expected to stay at home, look after a husband, and raise children. She craved love, but desired independence more. Each sister had their own idea of a perfect life. Margaret was living her dream; Eleanor was struggling to make her dreams come true.

Eleanor loathed listening to her sister chatter about the details of social events she attended and will be attending. Though she wanted to be a part of that world, she wanted to be the one everyone admired. Otherwise, her interest in social gatherings as a mere guest was contemptuous at best. After settling in and sipping tea with Margaret, Eleanor desperately tried to penetrate the conversation and change the subject from discussing formal attire worn at the fall festival to her reason for making the long trip to New Hampshire.

Shortly after her mother's death Margaret was put in

charge of her mother's affairs. Eleanor recalled her mother having a drug that she believed could help William. Margaret took a brief pause in the conversation to sip tea when Eleanor curiously asked Margaret if she kept her mother's container of medication after she passed. She believed a hallucinogen drug her mother once possessed was the answer to restoring William's nightmare.

Carefully Margaret sets her tea cup down on the polished table and without looking up, she quietly says, "It wasn't among mother's belongings."

Hearing the news, Eleanor tries not to look disappointed. Margaret interrupts Eleanor's thoughts, "I haven't seen any since we were children. Remember that soldier mother brought home?" Not waiting for Eleanor to respond, "She tried to ease his pain. The infection spread and she gave him the medicine to make the pain subside."

"Morphine," Eleanor briskly said.

"Yes, morphine. Mother held his hand and tried to comfort him. He passed in our living room, remember that? She was a good woman, rest her soul." Margaret turns away from Eleanor and stares out the window remembering the night her mother wept over a stranger dying in her arms. Eleanor places her hand over her sister's which still clutches the rested tea cup. Margaret looks down at Eleanor's hand and forces a smile. Eleanor gently pulls away as she replaces the memories of the soldier with William's despaired face.

Trying not to look desperate, Eleanor lowers her eyes, "Do you know where I could find some?"

Margaret studied Eleanor's delicate features. "Why? Are you in pain?"

Startled by her question. "No. I am in very good health but I believe it may help a dear friend of mine."

Curiosity and concern for her younger sister drove Margaret to ask a series of questions. Eleanor had an answer for every question, which eventually satisfied Margaret. By the end of the conversation Margaret agrees to find the drugs Eleanor needs for her friend.

As the week neared its end, Margaret's husband, Charles, supplied Eleanor with the drug she was looking for. When trying to acquire his source, Eleanor asked how he obtained the drug so quickly. She noticed he was uncomfortable and evaded the question before excusing himself. Later that day, Margaret explained to Eleanor that her husband's friend is a doctor and he supplies the medicine to help him cope with an old injury in his back. Margaret's expression fell into one of melancholy.

"Charles hasn't been the same," she says with a heavy heart. Margaret forces a smile and for the first time in her life, Eleanor sees how imperfect her perfect sister's life truly is.

Kissing her sister on the cheek, Margaret warns Eleanor, "Be careful with this, love." Shoving the warning to the back of her mind, she thanked her sister for allowing the visit and was on her way back to William.

Without much surprise, Eleanor discovered William in the exact position she had left him only now the room reeked of body odor and a thick scent of musk lingered in the air. His cheeks were sunken from weight loss and his eyes were dull and his skin was pale. It appeared as if he was slowly deteriorating to dust.

Eleanor kept the details of her visit to a minimum when she returned. She was very private when it came to her personal life. The relationship with Eleanor and her family had never been fully discussed with William. He tried to bring it up when they first met but the conversation was abruptly and bitterly ended by Eleanor.

Eleanor shared the good news of the drug and how it could help the hollowed man whose stress carved out his handsome features. Eleanor, understanding her job was no longer just an assistant, but to wholly care for William as if he were a child. She denied his request to take the drug until he had something in his stomach. She hurried off to make him frizzled ham and eggs.

To her surprise, William hadn't been bedridden the entire time during her brief absence; he had read and edited her story. This news filled her with pride and anticipation of his review. She could not believe he had pushed his anguish aside to read her manuscript. Anticipation of his review made it difficult to ignore the knots strangling her insides causing her to breathe rapidly.

To Eleanor's surprise, William quickly finished

eating and drinking the wine. This was her moment. It was time for the great William Warren to give her confirmation of her brilliant work. She took this opportunity to ask what his thoughts were on the manuscript. Those arrogant feelings of pride faded immediately. His flammable words charred her ego with an agonizing burn.

"The beginning was much too weak, the characters were incredibly shallow and underdeveloped, and the plot changed constantly. I also had some concerns regarding the ending. Did you forget to write an ending or were you undecided how it should end?" William's brutal honesty was not intended to offend Eleanor, she had asked for his honest review so he provided her one. He handed her the manuscript along with the empty plate and wine glass.

Eleanor, feeling defeated, paused in the hall after exiting William's study. Her eyes grazed the pages, each suggestion and edit stinging more than the last. William's picking apart and edits made the story hardly Eleanor's anymore. She sighed and looked up with damp eyes. Eleanor catches a glimpse of one of Williams's novels resting on the bookshelf between Mark Twain and Mary Shelley. An appropriate place for William's novel considering his works were as well known and appreciated. Cocking her head to the side, Eleanor uses one free hand to cover up the part of the binding on William's book with his name.

She smiled and whispered to herself, "Eleanor Price." She closed her eyes and envisioned the future. She would be a common topic amongst the most prestige and influential people of her time, perhaps her works would be mentioned in classrooms. The name, Eleanor Price, would live on even when she was long gone.

With a small smirk on her face she hurried to her bedroom.

Later that day, William complained to Eleanor that the dose she gave him had no effects and suggested a double dose. Eleanor made William wait until night to have his second dose of what he called "dream juice". She was never fond of needles, in fact, the injections made her quite queasy, but she braved through her discomfort for William's sake. She did not stick by him to witness whether or not it worked, feeling hurt by his lack of appreciation for her work, she left for bed.

The drug worked.

William was himself again, capturing each detail of his nightmares on the typewriter he loved so much. Every so often he would stop and think. This was a new behavior, he had never paused for more than an hour before and now he would stop for several. It did not matter much to him; he was thrilled the nightmares had returned and his newest masterpiece was in the works.

Weeks passed and the more William used the dream juice the less effective it became. His passion was his work, now it became more about the drug. Eleanor watched the transformation. The first few times she witnessed William taking more doses than the previous time she hadn't thought much of it. Besides, she was busy rewriting the story William had criticized so mercilessly. Now the supply was running dangerously low and the side effects were beginning to reveal themselves.

"Have you…um…is there any…" William tried to piece together a simple request but could not quite finish. He often seemed restless one moment and the next he could not find the strength to do even a simple task. He wore only long sleeves because the gruesome bruises that speckled his arms from the needle were too disturbing for Eleanor to stomach. The William Warren everyone had come to know and love was slipping away with every use. Rationalizing it to himself, William was convinced he was doing this for the greater good. Without his novels to entertain and for a moment make people feel like their problems did not matter would truly be letting everyone down. No one cared about the author. No one cared about their mental state. The real love came from storylines and characters the audience could relate to. That is his legacy. Those stories are his legacy. That drug is his legacy.

Soon the supply was gone and for the first time

in her life Eleanor watched William cry. Eleanor panicked and wrote to Margaret asking for more right away. The man known across the country as a creative genius was falling apart while his unknown associate did everything she could to keep him afloat. It was exhausting. It was unfair! She is the one responsible for keeping the ideas flowing, yet William is the one getting praised. Despite his criticisms, Eleanor knew she was a good writer, hell, she was great. Eleanor was clawing her way to the top and had plans to pass her mentor. She was growing impatient. Now was the time to make it happen.

"Margaret said she will send some right away!" Eleanor called to William when she received her sister's letter.

During the day beads of sweat rush down William's face despite his complaining of it being too cold. The once healthy man who had everything was watching it all slip away like sand in his fingers, desperate to create something out of his drug induced imagination. To William it did not matter how it worked or the toll it would take on him, so long as it was working.

The dream juice returned the nightmares in full force. Each shriek and moan that came from the awful creatures he dreamt about each night were amplified. As he brilliantly captured the nightmares in his latest novel; something else was starting to happen. His monsters were coming to life during his time awake!

Frequently Eleanor would find William shuffling purposelessly from room to room staring into the distance as if he were discovering the world for the first time. Evenings were the most difficult. William refused sleep on several occasions and insisted on staying up writing or daydreaming or just walking about. Insomnia was a growing trait that gifted him shadowy circles beneath his lifeless eyes. Before the nightmares were just that: nightmares. Now they had consumed all moments of both day and night for William and Eleanor.

Change was happening and it was happening expeditiously.

The shipment of dream juice could not have arrived sooner. It was around this time that William's publisher was attempting to make inquiries on a new piece of eminent horror to feed to the public. He was assured a masterpiece within months but during the brief period of withdrawals William had stopped writing entirely, in fact he could hardly function the way he used to. It was unnerving for Eleanor but quite exciting all at once knowing her vision of fame and fortune would come sooner than later.

The moment William laid eyes on the new shipment of dream juice things instantly became better. Once the drug was in his bloodstream the world seemed to spin in the right direction and Eleanor could breathe again. What was supposed to be an approximately three hundred page book now bordered on five hundred. Not only was William writing, he was writing faster, darker, and deeper. His words may be enchantingly haunting but with every fresh chapter he delved into, the nightmares seemed to crawl from their pages, moaning and shrieking and roaring. Once William hallucinated an entire room filled with these black creatures. They clawed at Williams's neck and wrapped themselves around him nearly suffocating their creator.

For weeks this would go on with Eleanor being the only anchor to reality William had. The constant reassurance of her presence turned sour as she too became engulfed in the twisted world of demons and hell fire William was living. Bringing him back to reality was as difficult as keeping the dream juice from his grasp.

Locked in his room for the third time within a week due to random fits of thrashing and screaming caused by the hallucinations, William plainly sits on the edge of his bed staring into emptiness. Eleanor's ear is pressed against the door, listening for a sign of life. As the silence drags on, moment of self-doubt ripples through her like a heavy stone tossed into a still pond. She had saved him, nurtured him, and brought out his full potential and purpose for this world. To some that would be a selfless act of raw human kindness, to

Eleanor those were the steps before the slaughter. In the eyes of Eleanor that was all William was at this moment, an animal being led to slaughter.

A day prior, Eleanor had slipped into William's office to examine the latest masterpiece he was about to grace the world with. As expected, it was nothing less than brilliant. Perfect, actually. Her patience was rendering quite thin with each day closing on the final chapter. Now was the time to execute the plot of her story and to write William's ending.

He could sense her presence. William shook with fear not because of the world his soul was living in, but because of the one he felt trapped in. Eleanor, the young woman he had shared secrets with, taught, cared for, was now the only monster he feared. In a way, the dream juice had given light to world around him instead of darkness; it allowed him to see what was truly happening. William saw that Eleanor was the true monster.

What could he do? His spirit and body were in two separate places while his mind was torn between the two. The only possible action to take was to wait to be smothered like a gentle flame by the one person he had completely trusted.

John Harris, the assistant editor of the publishing company and longtime friend of William grew anxious with the lack of correspondences.

He decided to pay an unexpected visit to William to check the progress of his latest work.

"I am afraid he is quite busy at the moment," Eleanor sweetly explains while keeping him from entering the house. "Perhaps another time?"

"I have traveled a long distance through the first snowfall to be here. If you would let me inside for moment I am sure Mr. Warren would be more than happy to see me."

"I am sure he would at another time but right now he does not want to see anyone; even me." Eleanor tried to sound convincing.

A loud pounding from William's bedroom startles both parties at the open door.

"What was that?" John questions. The pounding continues but this time it is followed by a deep voice crying out.

Shoving an unnerved Eleanor out of the way, John hurries to the source of the noise. He pauses a moment before throwing open the bedroom door. A body, yes, just a body tumbles onto him. The familiar spirit of William Warren was absent; the good friend John had come to know was now a thin, undernourished shell. The whites of his eyes were a murky gray and the once warm glow of William's skin had faded to a sickening pale, his features sunken. He let out another soul-piercing moan that would make the devil himself quake.

"My God!" John exclaims grasping to hold onto his fragile friend.

"What has happen to you, old friend?"

"I told him to stop!" Small tears rolled down Eleanor's cheeks, not from the grief of her mentor's condition, but from the crushing anxiety of being exposed. "He became addicted and I tried to stop him. He has been acting mad for nearly a month now!"

"Keep him here, I will send for a doctor." As John helped William back to his bed, his ankle is seized by bony claws that were once William's hands; the hands responsible for bringing imagination and provocative perspectives on death and the monsters we fear.

William's eyes were crusted with tears and his mouth quivered for the words to say to John, one of which was not to leave him with Eleanor. John reads this silent plea for help, so does Eleanor.

Before John has a chance to act on the unsettled feeling arising in his stomach, she grabs him by the arm urging him out the door. She could not care less if John came back with help for William, there was only one chapter left to complete in the novel. By this point William was no longer of use. The plan was to leave him here to either rot or let the dream juice take him to a permanent nightmare. An asylum would work just as well. John was unsure of the severity of his friend's condition but Eleanor knew he was already gone.

News of the famed author William Warren being

committed after tragically losing his mind swept the country. His friends and family consoled each other and tried to understand what went wrong. All of that talent wasted at such a young age. Imagine the stories he could have written, the inspiration he could have given if only he had not resorted to drugs. If only he had been more careful, if only...

It was meant to remain a secret but soon the public learned that William Warren had been committed to the asylum. As rumors spread throughout the city, Eleanor kept herself busy writing the ending to William's novel. A story this brilliant is beyond even William's talent; the dream juice gave him more than nightmares, it cursed him with a hellish reality making the nightmares seem like sweet daydreams.

The novel utterly terrified Eleanor.

When the time had come for Eleanor to submit *her* story something seemed to bubble within her. Was it shame? Guilt? Possibly, although she did not pay much mind to such emotions; after all, her ticket to everything she has ever wanted lies within the pages upon pages of fresh nightmares sure to capture and tease the dark parts of the minds of her soon to be adoring fans.

Eleanor waited for what seemed like years for a response from the publishing company who were still in shock over William's mental condition and admittance to the asylum. Finally the letter from the publishing company arrived. She read each word out loud as if she were being honored for the fine work submitted. They loved it, they yearned for it, and they feared it. There was one miniscule note added to the never ending pile of compliments: change the ending. The company said it was far too boring and left the audience perplexed as to what happened to the characters and the writing seemed to turn sour during the last chapter. Within the month they expected a new-and much improved-ending.

Panic set in as her eyes raked over the words again and again. A new ending? Sure Eleanor could provide them with another ending but with the scathing reviews of her only contribution to the novel it was apparent William was still needed to finish it. That was not the part that vexed her, the most difficult part of the editor's feedback was the confirmation that she could not and would not match William's talent. Everything she had believed about herself burned down around her until the ashes of her reality buried her. It was enough to drive her mad.

With every passing day, the crushing weight of the

deadline filled her with anxiety; finally she was struck with an idea. If she could not create her own ending why not return it to the original owner to finish? William understood these fantasies better than his own reality and would surely put these demons on the page to rest. Closure was one of the most valued things to William, he could not leave a story in its midst. And from this idea Eleanor conjured a new plan.

It was not easy to see William in such a corroded state. Eleanor never fully understood what she had put him through until her visit to the asylum. He was no longer hostile or frantic; in fact he spent most of his days in solitude in the corner of the common room, according to the nurse who allowed Eleanor a quick visitation.

Eleanor's authoritative walk was halted and a gasp escaped her mouth when she laid her eyes on his hunched body in an old creaky chair in the corner of the common room.

She sat beside him and nodded to the nurse to give them privacy. The nurse smiled and said she would return shortly. Eleanor stared at his fragile body for a few minutes but could not bring herself to make eye contact. The only sign of life was his chest moving shallowly to pump oxygen through the shell he had become and his eyes staring straight ahead. She gave him the message the editors had given to her and the predicament this had placed her in. The sweet temptation of closure to his final masterpiece, the last words of his career had been offered to him on a silver platter. Eleanor waited for William to give her what she wanted. This is it, the ending will be complete and the credit would be hers! Everything was so close she could nearly hear the praise from the publishers, the public, and her sister. It was all so close.

A creak in the chair made Eleanor jump as William turned his head to her. His eyes reminded her of melting glaciers, once concrete and magnificent but have turned into nothing but melting slush. For a single moment Eleanor saw a glimpse of the great William Warren spark back to life when he appeared to recognize her. With a knowing smirk and a tiny shake of his head Eleanor's world was sent into flames. William soaked up every single second of her internal collapse as he watched her leave the common room in a daze allowing him the greatest closure he could have asked for. Eleanor's dream that was so close was slipping and there was nothing she could do.

Sleep deprived, hungry, fueled by anger and time, Eleanor wiped away the seemingly endless tears from her bloodshot eyes. With only days to submit the ending for the novel; she panicked. In fact, that was the only thing she could identify with, everything and everyone seemed to disintegrate over time. Then an idea came to her, there was still some dream juice left, enough, she thought, to bring her own nightmares to life.

In a desperate attempt to make the deadline lurking above her head, Eleanor allowed herself a larger dose of the dream juice than William had taken. More nightmares equal more inspiration, right? If she could see and understand the things William had the pages would practically write themselves. Much to Eleanor's dismay the dream juice guided her into a world with molasses time and misplaced colors. This was not right. Where were the monsters? The demons? The twisted reality he had so willingly launched himself into was nonexistent but Eleanor would not accept it.

Again and again she allowed herself to slip under the dream juice's influence but never fully entered the world William now resided in forever. The bruises on her arm from the needle were constant reminders of her failure. On occasion her heart would race when she heard a thump or saw a shadow move out of the corner of her eye but nothing near the severity of what she had anticipated. Each time she would use the dream juice she would increase the dosage but could never quite get the desired results.

Her heart began to race, her palms sweated, and the world seemed to cave in. Darkness covered everything and Eleanor fell to the floor.

John Harris had taken a leave of absence from the publishing company to stay by William's side after he was institutionalized. The two friends spent a majority of their time in silence, sometimes on a good day, William would have brief conversations that didn't quite make sense to his friend. John was by William's side religiously for three weeks until he was requested back by the publishing company. Even then he would make trips as often as possible to give any sort of comfort and sense of hope to William that he could.

Flames singed Eleanor's body; the distressing moans of tortured souls surrounded her. She was not moving but an ever present illusion of falling churned within her. There was one voice above all others Eleanor could not recognize. It was not a reassuring voice or one she thought she would ever hear. What was this? Where was she? Hell? Oh God, no. She could not be dead, not now. Not before she left her fingerprint on the world. Before she met the source of the crackling voice she, in turn, let out her own eternal cry.

Eleanor's death made the local newspaper. She had gotten what she always desired, recognition. Although the details of her death were in print for all to see and gossip about, William overshadowed Eleanor once again with his own death. He died the day after her making headlines throughout the country. William passed peacefully in his sleep, the only place where he was able to escape the nightmare that had become his reality.

Printed in the United States
By Bookmasters